The Little Deer of the Florida Keys

In Loving Memory of my Mother

The Little Deer of the Florida Keys

WRITTEN AND PHOTOGRAPHED BY

HOPE RYDEN

G. P. PUTNAM'S SONS NEW YORK

Acknowledgments

I wish to thank Don Kosin, manager of the National Key Deer Refuge, for help and information cheerfully given during the two seasons I tracked deer in the lower keys. I am also grateful to refuge personnel, Frank Duke and Dorothea (Deedee) Moorman, for interesting discussions and suggestions.

To Jack Watson, former manager of the National Key Deer Refuge, I am indebted for having saved the deer when its population was critically low. His recollections were invaluable to me in reconstructing the history of the Refuge—as were those of Charles Brookfield, former Florida representative for the National Audubon Society.

Without the friendships of many residents of Big Pine Key, I might not have succeeded in obtaining some of the behavioral photographs that appear in this book. Peg and Gene Riepi, "Mimo" and Larue Sellers and Mr. and Mrs. Arthur Merrell not only gave me access to their property, they faithfully reported to me on the movements of deer in their respective areas.

I am indebted to *National Audubon Magazine* for financing one season of my field work.

Behaviorial studies conducted by William D. Klimstra, N.J. Silvy and James W. Hardin greatly helped me understand the deer interactions I observed.

The cartoon by the late J.N. "Ding" Darling, which appears on page 11, did much to rally support for the cause of the vanishing deer. I am grateful to his estate for permission to reproduce it.

A special thanks to Modernage Photo Lab for prompt and reliable film reports while I was in the field.

 Published simultaneously in Canada by Longman Canada Limited, Toronto. Printed in the United States of America

Library of Congress Cataloging in Publication Data Ryden, Hope. The little deer of the Florida Keys. SUMMARY: Discusses the characteristics, natural environment, and the threatened survival of the species of small deer living on the Florida Keys. 1. White-tailed deer—Juvenile literature. 2. Mammals—Florida—Florida Keys—Juvenile literature. [1. White-tailed deer. 2. Mammals—Florida—Florida Keys. 3. Wildlife conservation] I. Title.
QL737.U55R9 599'.7357 77-20884
ISBN 0-399-20635-3

In America there lives a small deer no bigger than a large dog. It is one of the loveliest creatures in all the world. Yet many Americans are unfamiliar with its existence. Only a generation ago, it was so rarely seen that many people believed it had become extinct.

This little deer is called a key deer because it is found only on small islands, called keys, off the tip of Florida. These islands are green and beautiful. Warm seas surround them. Overhead a blue sky mirrors the water. On it, enormous clouds build up, sometimes rising to great heights before they float away like gigantic schooners.

The islands are a tropical paradise. Trees with poetic names like gumbo limbo, towering ficus and wild acacia grow here and lock their branches in thick forests, called hammocks. In other places, vegetation is less dense. Stands of pines admit shafts of light that warm the lowly palmettos at their feet. And, along the shores of these islands are found the most wonderful trees of all. Red mangroves stand high on tangles of prop roots that grow above the ground.

Like the enchanted forest that surrounded Sleeping Beauty's castle, mangrove trees protect the beautiful keys they encircle. The savage force of hurricanes that blow in suddenly from the sea is weakened by a mangrove thicket of branches and roots. In centuries past, raiding pirates could not navigate ships through such a snarl of trees. And more recently, hunters intent on killing the key deer that inhabit these islands were thwarted when the little creatures took shelter in a maze of curved roots.

Raccoon

In this island setting, it seems strange to encounter any kind of deer at all, least of all one that is so small. Tropical birds adorn the trees. That seems appropriate. Gigantic alligators wallow in the sink holes that pock the islands. They belong. Even the uncommonly pale raccoons that chase each other from treetop to treetop, quarreling like noisy squirrels, do not seem out of place here. But little deer!

White ibis

American alligator

How did they get here? Why are they so small? How do they survive in such a marinelike environment? What are their habits? And why do we Americans know so little about this animal that is unique to our land?

Some of these questions have intrigued visitors to the keys since the little deer was first sighted by a crew member on Columbus's fourth voyage. He wrote about it in the ship's log. Fifty years later a Spanish sailor named Hernando d'Escalante Fontenada got a closer look at one. Given the circumstances, he no doubt would have preferred to pass up the opportunity. A tropical storm wrecked Fontenada's ship on a barrier reef that runs parallel to the Florida keys. He swam ashore, where he was taken prisoner by the Calusa Indians. For seventeen years Fontenada was enslaved by this fierce tribe, and during that period he kept a diary. In one entry he described the little deer that dwells on the islands, calling it "a great wonder."

But not everyone is capable of perceiving "a great wonder." So it was that in the 19th century, when the Florida keys began to be settled, the dainty little key deer was heedlessly slaughtered. For, unlike the Calusa Indians, who took from nature only what they needed, the settlers took all that they could get. To these pioneers, wildlife seemed to be in unlimited supply.

So roseate spoonbills went into stewpots. White-crowned pigeons were hunted almost to extinction. The great sea turtles that had dwelt in the green shallows since time immemorial were all but wiped out. And the vulnerable little key deer, no bigger than some of the hunting dogs that were set upon them, were driven by the score into the surrounding seas where they could easily be shot.

THE SMALLEST SPECIES OF DEER IN NORTH AMERICA, ALONE, UNGUARDED AND ON THE WAY OUT!

This goading cartoon by J. N. "Ding" Darling aroused the public.

Moreover, as the years passed, many of the emerald gems in that long necklace of islands that dangles from Florida's tip were permanently scarred by dredging, burning, filling, lumbering, and construction. So, by the middle of the present century, much of the deers' habitat had been taken by man. Deer were found only on a few keys some 100 miles southwest of the mainland. And even here they were seldom seen.

Some people began to suspect they were only a legend. Like stories of sixteenth century pirate ships said to have foundered offshore. But neither the treasure ships nor the deer herds were myths. Wreckage of sixteenth-century schooners, still visible beneath the clear waters, bore witness to the age of piracy. And whitened, cast-off antlers, relics of bygone buck fights, littered the hammocks and piney woods and confirmed the past existence of countless generations of a small-sized deer.

But this small-sized deer was seldom seen anymore. No one could guess how many might still be savoring the salty leaves of the red mangrove on keys with names like Knockemdown, Cudjoe, Big Pine, Torch and No Name. At the close of World War Two, some optimistic people thought there still might be some fifty deer scattered across a few uninhabited islands. Others worried that a buck killed on the newly built highway that crossed Big Pine Key was the last of its kind.

But there were still those who knew how to find the few deer that remained. They went by night to hunt them, using spotlights to pick up the shine of an eye. When caught in a bright beam, the deer would freeze in its tracks, making itself an easy target. If the men missed their mark, they returned the following day, set fire to the trees, and flushed the panicked animal into the sea, where it could easily be picked off.

In 1939 a state regulation had been hastily passed which prohibited the hunting of the vanishing deer. But that law was ignored. It is hardly surprising. Even when hunters were caught red-handed with slain deer in their possession, local judges let them off.

In some ways the poachers behaved as if the lower keys were still a lawless frontier. They imitated a style of life that in times past had been necessary, but which no longer made sense.

The first settlers on the Florida keys had been a hardy lot. They had to be in order to endure the isolation, to survive the devastating hurricanes, and not to succumb to the clouds of mosquitoes and sand flies that breed here. They lived off the sea and took from the land whatever it would give.

Understandably, their descendants were proud of their pioneer heritage and wanted to be as self-sufficient and as independent as their forebears. But times had changed. No longer was it necessary, or even possible, to live off the land. A highway now connected 130 miles of keys to the mainland of Florida. Produce could be shipped to the islands daily. Locally, resources had become scarce. Too many people had used up too much of nature's bounty too quickly. Unless the remaining wild places and uninhabited outer islands could be protected, soon there would be no more deer, no more wading birds, no more bald eagles, no more tropical paradise.

Still, the men who went by night to hunt the key deer fancied themselves to be acting in the same spirit as their pioneer ancestors. So they continued to hunt and kill the last of the key deer, not out of necessity, but to satisfy some yearning for a bygone time.

But there were other residents of the keys who cherished their surroundings. They wanted to protect the things that made island living so delightful. They enjoyed watching an osprey dive for a fish. They appreciated the sight of a tree hung with wild orchids. They tried to keep hunters away from those wild places that might still be sheltering deer. It was a time of conflict.

One visitor to the keys, an eleven-year-old boy named Gary Allen, was among the first to call attention to the plight of the key deer. In 1947 he wrote to President Truman and later to President Eisenhower, describing the "phantom" creature that nobody saw anymore. He wrote to United States senators and congressmen. He wrote to newspaper editors. He wrote to scout groups. And in all his letters he suggested that the federal government set aside land for the vanishing deer. Perhaps, given help, their numbers would increase.

But the fight to save the key deer was not quickly won. As people across the nation became interested in the cause, scientist and conservationist lined up against politician and land speculator. Neighbor argued with neighbor. Time and time again bills were introduced in Congress to set up just such a key deer sanctuary as Gary Allen had envisioned. But time and time again these bills were defeated.

Meanwhile, what deer remained were keeping out of sight. No doubt these survivors were the shyest of their kind. How else had they eluded the notice of the poachers who continued to hunt them?

As they had done over the ages, does continued to drop their fawns in secret places. A newborn fawn is hard to see. Its spots blend with the dapples of sunlight that penetrate the treetops. When a person or animal comes near, a fawn will drop to the ground and remain as motionless as a stone. Approached too closely, the spotted "stone" may suddenly come to life and bound off. But the fawn will soon hide again. And chances are slight that it will be discovered a second time. It is difficult to see a fawn in the kaleidoscope of light and shadow that plays upon a forest floor.

Besides, a very young fawn spends much of its early life alone. It is safer for it to do so. Survival depends upon its ability to remain hidden. A doe is more visible than a fawn and, when the two are together, her presence only calls attention to its existence. So, when a mother deer makes the rounds of her favorite feeding places, she leaves her new baby behind in a special range she has chosen for it. She permits no other deer to intrude on this area.

People who happen upon a young fawn by itself in the woods sometimes make the mistake of thinking the little one has been orphaned or is abandoned. Should these well-meaning but misguided persons decide to take it home, they will create an unresolvable problem for themselves and much misery for the baby and its mother. Once separated from the doe, a fawn has no opportunity to learn to fend for itself. So later, when it must be released, it will probably not survive. Moreover, there is no sight more pathetic than that of a doe searching for her baby. At first she will bleat softly. If her fawn does not respond with a soft mewling sound, the doe will begin to bellow. Does have been known to call for their missing young for as long as two weeks before giving up the search.

During those hours of daylight and darkness that a doe does spend with her new baby, she is very alert. If she suspects somebody or something is lurking nearby, she signals her fawn by raising her tail. When the baby sees this "white flag" go up, it prepares to drop to the ground or gets ready to bound for

cover. Meanwhile, its mother stands warily with one leg poised in the air, ready to drum the ground in a second alert. As she tries to pick up the scent of the threat, she may drag so deeply on the air that her head will bob up and down like a hobby horse. Sometimes she will snort to clear her nostrils and so get a better reading of the air. Failing to identify the cause or direction of the threat, she may simply bleat to her baby to head for cover.

Does are wonderful mothers. It is apparent to those who have watched a mother deer that she feels a strong attachment to her fawn. Each time they are reunited, the two run together and greet with much licking and tail wagging. After the baby has nursed, it capers about and may even entice its mother into a game of chase. It is not unusual for a doe to play with her fawn. For that matter, it is not unusual for two grown does to play with each other.

Frequently, a doe will give birth to twins. However, key deer have fewer twins than do the larger subspecies of whitetail deer that live on the mainland. When twins do occur, they support each other in many ways. They lick and clean one another. They play together. And they even alert each other to danger by raising their little flaglike tails and stomping their tiny hoofs. The hoofprint of a newborn key fawn is about the size of a person's thumbnail. So it is doubtful that their drumming produces much effect.

Any strange doe or buck that enters a young fawn's special range can expect trouble. Should the baby's mother spy the intruder, she will chase it away. A mother deer does not lack courage. She can even rout a buck much larger than herself. And if the trespasser doesn't depart quickly enough to suit her, she will rise on her hind legs and strike him with her sharp forefeet.

It seems a miracle of timing that bucks should lose their antlers in March, just before the new fawns are born in the spring. Without headgear, a buck is no match for a mother deer. In fact, after his rack falls off, a buck's head is very sensitive. His new antlers, which sprout quickly, are covered with delicate skin, called velvet. When a doe stands on her hind legs as if to strike this part of a buck's head, he will back away in a hurry. Later, in the fall, after his antlers have grown back, he will be more aggressive and can easily dominate any doe he encounters. But by that time the fawns no longer need so much maternal protection. Nearly all of them will have lost their spots. Male fawns will be showing small buttons where their antlers are already beginning to develop. And some buck fawns will even be quite independent.

But many weeks of spring and summer will have to pass before the mating season brings this new social order to the deer herd. Meanwhile, a fawn spends increasing periods of time following its mother about, learning from her example.

Gradually, a mother doe extends the boundaries of her baby's range, leading it to new sources of food and water. While she munches on succulent leaves and fruits, her curious little one will sniff the contents of her mouth. In so doing it learns which foods are palatable.

Experience also can be a teacher. A noseful of thorns is a painful lesson, one not soon forgotten. Still, imitating mother is a less hazardous way to learn. So nature, which programs all creatures for survival, has provided fawns with an experienced model to follow. Does and fawns remain together for at least one year.

As her baby grows stronger, a mother doe becomes less aggressive toward other deer. By the time her fawn is six weeks old, she is ready to rejoin those does that make up her own special band. These are her lifetime companions, whom she has

temporarily deserted to devote full time to her newborn. Many of them will have given birth, too. Now they reunite. Their babies meet. A new pattern of life emerges.

Summer is a sociable time for does and fawns. Fawns caper and chase one another about. Does relax in the shade, chewing their cuds and looking for all the world like talkative nannies. Cattle egrets flit among them, lighting as gracefully as long-legged ballerinas dressed in white. The showy birds pick ticks and flies from the backs of their docile hosts. All is serene. Only the anxious bleat of a baby, momentarily strayed, adds a plaintive note to the tranquil scene.

But even in summer the mother doe requires solitude. In this respect, key deer differ from other subspecies. They are more often found by themselves. Perhaps the recollection of a favorite berry bush is the lure. Or perhaps the doe simply seeks a few hours of privacy. Her baby will either be dropped off in its former range or left in the care of her companions. In the latter case, it will be well looked after. In fact, so solicitious are does toward any fawn in their band, it is sometimes difficult to ascertain which ones are the real mothers.

Soon enough the rambler will rejoin her companions. The reunion will be occasion for a greeting ritual. Nose-touching reassures members that she is no stranger. Grooming and licking follow. Like a baby, the object of all the attention submits to her wet reception. An onlooker could never doubt the experience is a pleasurable one for her.

A typical band of does is made up of an old "lead" doe, some of her female offspring from previous years, and all their new fawns. (Here the lead doe still wears the radio collar that allowed scientists to track her movements over a period of years.) Rarely will the group exceed nine adult animals. A band of females remains intact for years. Members know and recognize one another, greet and groom one another, and provide one another with a baby-sitting service.

By contrast, males do not form bands. Two or three bucks may on occasion feed together, but their association is temporary. Or sometimes, an adult male will pay a visit to one of the female bands. If he is the grown son or a twin of one of the does, he will be tolerated. Even so, he will not remain among them long. His body dictates that he follow a different life-style.

As early as July, a buck's antlers may be fully formed. But they will still be covered with velvet. Not until September will this sensitive skin begin to peel away, hanging in loose strips like Spanish moss from his forked branches. At this stage a buck will feel uncomfortable. In fact, he will be in a frenzy to rid himself of the loose and itchy skin. Tree trunks will be butted and branches broken in an effort to gain relief. For about a week in September, the cleaning and the polishing of his antlers will be his single preoccupation. Finally, though, he will be rewarded by a clean and burnished rack. Thus arrayed, and with neck well limbered, a buck is ready to enter the aggressive phase of his cyclical life. His shyness vanishes.

Now it is the turn of the male to dominate. Whereas does are belligerent in spring when their babies are young, in fall bucks have their way. This is the mating season when males are "on the fight."

A buck fight is a terrible sight to witness. Two males battling over a female may mortally wound each other. Combatants circle, snort, and paw the ground for several minutes before they lower their heads and ram into each other at top speed like two colliding trains. Sometimes their clanking antlers be-

come locked together, and as a result the two animals die of starvation. Of course, there is a purpose behind their aggressive behavior. Only the most powerful bucks triumph and sire the new fawns. This ensures the next generation will inherit strength.

During the mating season males are said to be "in rut" and are very restless and cantankerous. Not only do they fight one another, they chase and harass any half-grown fawns accompanying their mothers. Many young deer are run onto roads. In late fall highway fatalities are high.

Even adult does are rudely herded and chased by males in rut. When an amorous buck fixes his attention on a particular female, he may attach himself to her band and run her about until she is forced to leave the group. Then the chase really begins. For two or three days the animals may be seen racing through the woods at top speed. Finally, when the female is ready to mate, she will stop running. The pair will then remain together for one or two days before the male departs to seek another female ready for his peculiar form of courtship.

A would-be suitor locates a doe in heat by trailing. That is, he travels through the woods with his nose to the ground like some kind of animated vacuum cleaner. While trailing, a buck is oblivious to everything else in the world. It is even possible for a person to get quite close to him at this time. But should this preoccupied male encounter a rival, he will quickly become aroused. Unless one buck indicates that he accepts defeat in advance, the two will fight. But if one male is clearly the weaker of the two, he very likely will avoid deadly combat by averting his head and flattening his ears.

In March, after they have shed their antlers, all bucks are equals. Like Samson after his haircut, male deer lose their power with the loss of their headgear. For the next few months, while their new racks are sprouting, they live solitary lives and avoid conflict. The timing of this mood change is nothing short of elegant. It corresponds with the birth of the fawns.

Each year a buck grows a bigger rack. The antlers of a yearling are simple spikes. A two-year-old buck usually sports two points, or tines, on each antler. By age three, antler development slows down. A key deer buck whose antlers bear four tines is probably more than four and may be as old as nine.

The antlers of aging deer often grow in a deformed shape.

At six, a buck is past his prime and will rarely challenge another male to battle. By the same token, bucks under age two stay out of the way of males age three to five who are at the height of their power. And while yearlings may appear to fight one another, their sparring matches are actually only practice bouts. Rarely is any damage done.

One threat that is common to all key deer, young and old, male and female, is drought. Salt water surrounds their island home, but there is little fresh water to drink. During the dry season, from December to April, deer often swim from key to key searching for pockets of fresh water to relieve their thirst. As a consequence, this subspecies has become a powerful swimmer. Individuals unable to ford strong ocean currents did not live to contribute their incompetence to the herd. That is how natural selection works.

One island, named Big Pine Key, contains water the year round. Its underlying oolite rock is pocked with holes which retain the rain that falls during the wet season. For this reason, Big Pine Key is the most important of all islands presently used by key deer. During a drought, large numbers of animals congregate here.

But land on Big Pine Key is also prized by human beings, who like to live here too. Houses and canals have been built alongside wild tracts that are home to many key deer. Fortunately, present day residents of Big Pine Key are proud of the

rare animal that lives among them. Some residents even encourage deer to visit their yards, luring them out of the woods with cabbage leaves, fruit rinds, and carrots. As a result, a few have become tame and even take food from a familiar hand.

But this peaceable kingdom did not always exist. During the 1950s a group of people in the keys resisted every plan to create the National Key Deer Refuge. In this they were led by real estate developers who, at the close of World War Two, were busy converting wilderness tracts into housing divisions.

These land speculators wanted no limit put on their business ventures. So they generated local opposition to the refuge idea by telling residents of the lower keys that, in order to create it, the government would seize private property. Not surprisingly, home owners reacted emotionally.

Moreover, many people questioned the necessity of protecting an animal as commonplace and as widely distributed as is the deer. They failed to realize that the creature that lived in the Florida keys was unlike any other deer in the world. And when they were told, some people refused to believe it.

The size of the deer became an issue. Were they really smaller than other subspecies of whitetail deer found elsewhere in the United States? Were they really special enough to warrant the trouble and sacrifice it would take to save them?

Since they were so seldom seen, it was not easy to know. True, a buck recently struck by a car had measured no bigger than a collie dog. But some people argued that it might have been a young animal. Others recalled having seen key deer in years past that appeared to be no different from deer found on the mainland.

Oddly, when sighted from afar, a key deer doesn't look as small as it actually is. Even in photographs, the illusion of greater size is created, in part, by the unusual plant life that forms the animal's backdrop. It is difficult to judge the height of the little palmetto or the silver thatch palm beside which a deer might be standing. These trees could be mistaken for taller varieties of palms. In that event, the deer itself would appear to be very large indeed. The eye is easily deceived. To accurately estimate the size of an animal, one must see it alongside a familiar figure, such as a dog or a person.

To answer the argument about size, therefore, scientific evidence was examined. Many years earlier, when key deer were still numerous, two mammalogists named Glover Allen and Thomas Barbour measured and weighed a number of them. Their specimens proved to be considerably smaller than other subspecies of the Virginia whitetail deer.

For example, whitetail bucks living in Maine usually weigh over 200 pounds and may even grow to weigh 300 pounds. This subspecies is named *Odocoileus virginianus borealis.* In New York and Pennsylvania, bucks belonging to another subspecies of whitetail deer, called *Odocoileus virginianus virginianus,* range in weight from 150 to 200 pounds. Somewhat smaller are the deer that live on the Florida mainland. They are called *Odocoileus virginianus osceola.* Males weigh between 110 and 155 pounds. But the key deer is decidedly the smallest deer in North America. Bucks range in weight from 80 to 110 pounds, less than some breeds of dog. Females are considerably smaller. Some full-grown does do not exceed 35 pounds! Barbour and Allen gave this subspecies the Latin name *Odocoileus virginianus clavium.*

But to those who opposed the creation of a deer refuge, this scientific study was not persuasive. They objected that Barbour and Allen had not collected a sufficient number of examples. And since Barbour and Allen were no longer around to defend their work, the matter was not easily resolved.

Then a local citizen by the name of Wallace Kirke decided to conduct his own research. He scoured the woods for old deer skulls and compared them to skulls belonging to northern deer.

Not only did he find them to be the smallest of any type in North America, he confirmed other differences. He noted that the tooth row of the key deer was unique. Antler formation was special, too. Kirke claimed that, blindfolded, he could pick out a key deer skull from a pile of deer skulls, just by feeling it.

But how did these physical differences happen to arise? And even more curious, how did this little animal come to be in the Florida keys in the first place?

Both of these questions can be answered by a single explanation. Many thousands of years ago, when the last ice age was coming to an end, melting glaciers caused the seas to rise. As a consequence, a long peninsula that extended from the tip of Florida into the Gulf of Mexico was flooded. Only the highest points of this peninsula remained above water. These became the chain of islands known today as the Florida keys.

Deer were marooned here, and these animals had to adapt to a radically altered environment or perish. Some did die. Only those able to cope with the hazards of island life survived to pass on their traits to the generations that followed. They became powerful swimmers. They evolved a salt tolerance equal to that of sheep. They grew smaller and, as most people agree, prettier. Behavioral changes occurred. Deer here could afford to be more independent than could their mainland cousins. Here there was no need to constantly herd together for protection

from wildcats, wolves, and bears, for no such land predators existed. On the other hand, drought, hurricanes, sharks, and crocodiles were menaces that demanded different responses from the stranded deer.

While any or all of the above characteristics made this deer unique, its reduced size captured the public imagination. Opponents of the deer refuge realized this. A little deer is irresistible. So this was the characteristic they tried to refute. Like medieval scholars pointlessly debating how many angels can sit on the head of a pin, people argued about the size of the unseen deer. Meanwhile, the animal itself was poised on the abyss of extinction.

Some biologists feared numbers had already fallen too low for the herd to make a recovery. When death rate exceeds birth rate, a species cannot be saved. And while poachers continued to kill every deer they could locate, nobody dared hope how many does might still be giving birth to young.

Obviously, immediate action was called for or there would be no animals left to enjoy the hotly contested deer refuge. Two conservation organizations took the initiative. The Boone and Crockett Club of New York City and the National Wildlife Federation contributed money to pay a United States warden who was employed at the nearby Great White Heron Refuge to extend his patrol to include the deer habitat as well. This man's name was Jack Watson.

If ever there was a friend to key deer, it was Jack Watson. By day and by night he tramped wilderness areas, watching and waiting for poachers to appear. His was a rough assignment. Tangles of mangroves made moving about difficult. Crocodiles and poisonous snakes were a constant threat. But hardly more so than were the poachers he was tracking, who fired on Watson, tried to run him down with a car, and in every conceivable way attempted to scare him off.

But Watson would not be intimidated. He, in fact, proved to be every bit as tough as the men he pursued. When he found hidden in the woods a vehicle that contained an empty gun rack, he would lie in wait for the poachers' return. If armed men showed up, bearing the evidence of their crime, he would step from the brush and singlehandedly arrest them all.

Out of sheer respect for this fearless warden, judges began taking the offense of poaching seriously. They handed down stiff sentences to the men Watson brought before them. At last the key deer had an effective defender.

As poaching came under control, the deer slowly began to multiply. Now the need for a permanent refuge became imperative. And not only to preserve deer. The same mangrove thickets and hammocks that sheltered key deer also provided homes for thirteen other endangered species.

These were:
the southern bald eagle,
the great white heron,
(opposite)
the reddish egret,
the roseate spoonbill,
the mangrove cuckoo,
the West Indian nighthawk,
the eastern pelican,
the American osprey,
the white-crowned pigeon,
the green turtle,
the key blacksnake,
the American alligator and
the American crocodile.

The outlook for all these creatures did not appear hopeful. During the 1950s, three bills to preserve their priceless habitat were sent to Congress. Three times Congress voted the legislation down. Ten years had passed since eleven-year-old Gary Allen first called attention to the plight of the key deer. Gary was now a grown man. And still the deer had no permanent home.

Fortunately, two United States congressmen from Florida refused to accept defeat. In 1957, for a fourth time, representatives Dante Fascell and Charles Bennett introduced legislation to create a deer refuge. Supporters of the bill realized this would be their last chance to save the key deer. Should Congress again vote down the measure, the slowly reviving herd would surely be swallowed up by "progress."

It was commonly known that one powerful politician from the lower keys stood in the way of the bill's passage. Not only did he incite others to oppose the refuge, he also succeeded in intimidating many who favored it. As a result, members of Congress got a false picture of the situation. They believed that the majority of people who lived in the Florida keys did not want a deer refuge to be established there. And they prepared to vote accordingly.

Actually, when the facts were finally made known, the opposite turned out to be true. Most of the people who lived in the Florida keys favored the idea of a deer refuge. But either they had neglected to speak up or they refrained from doing so for fear of reprisals. Now it was imperative that everyone stand up and be counted.

Deer supporters went into action. Members of the Audubon Society mounted a door-to-door campaign to obtain signatures on refuge petitions. They also urged residents of the keys to write their congressmen and express support for the deer refuge. Conservationists spoke before civic groups and asked them to draw up resolutions in favor of the refuge bill. Newspapers carried stories about the vanishing deer. Children helped. Scout groups organized letter-writing campaigns. Word spread. In a short time people across the nation were involved. Congress was inundated with letters.

There is probably no more effective way to promote the cause of conservation than by writing one's elected representatives. Congressmen are accustomed to hearing from powerful companies that lobby in their own self-interest. But when ordinary Americans spontaneously rally behind a cause, legislators sit up and take notice. After all, it is the duty of elected officials to carry out the will of the people.

By the time hearings on the bill were held in Washington, D.C., in July of 1957, congressmen were not in doubt how people felt about key deer. Their mail had run 200 to 1 in favor of the refuge. In addition, they had received petitions containing thousands of names, which urged passage of the bill.

Even the politician who had blocked all previous legislation realized he was powerless to override the wishes of so many citizens. He withdrew his objections, the opposition collapsed, and the legislation passed. After a decade of strife, the National Key Deer Refuge was finally established.

Today key deer number several hundred and enjoy a 7,000-acre refuge that includes all or parts of eighteen keys. Only a few of these islands are also inhabited by people. Those that are not have been permanently reserved for animals and will remain forever wild.

Nevertheless, the key deer is not quite "saved." Until 2,500 animals can be counted, *Ocodoileus virginianus clavium* will continue to be listed as an endangered species. So the United States Fish and Wildlife Service continues to take every precau-

tion to protect the key deer. It is now a serious crime punishable by a $20,000 fine to harass or kill a key deer.

Even so, new threats to this subspecies have developed. A number of deer have chosen to establish ranges on non-refuge land which is still in a wild state, but which is scheduled for development. When building begins on this privately owned property, the resident animals will certainly suffer a setback. Other obstacles also stand in the way of the key deer's total recovery. Today 78 percent of all known deer losses are caused by road accidents. Pet dogs, too, menace the bands. And in recent years, there has been a recurrence of poaching. A team of biologists who tagged and studied key deer over a five-year period concluded that as a result of these factors, the herd may never attain the desired population level of 2,500 animals.

But even if this ideal number is not achieved, the phantom deer of the Florida keys has made a remarkable comeback. With continued protection, the species will no doubt survive. And thanks to the efforts of the dedicated people who fought to provide it a refuge, so will the white-crowned pigeon, the mangrove cuckoo, and many other rare and endangered species.

No animal can exist without a suitable place to live. If mankind continues to convert all wilderness to his own use, he will ultimately find himself a lonely inhabitant on a barren planet. On the other hand, if he, like the people of the Florida keys, decides to leave part of the world for those creatures who came before him, his own life will be enriched.

Today the lower Florida keys remain green and beautiful. And they still harbor a most improbable and rare creature. A deer no bigger than a large dog.

Hope Ryden's love and understanding of animals and nature go back to her childhood. She grew up in western Illinois and spent summers in the forested regions of northern Wisconsin.

A writer and producer of documentary films, Ms. Ryden was also feature producer for the ABC Evening News from 1966 to 1968. Her nature films include "Operation Gwamba," an on-the-scene report of the rescue of 10,000 wild animals from a flooded jungle in South America. In 1975, while producing a film on coastal wetlands for Public Broadcasting System, she noticed the little deer of the Florida Keys. After completing "The Wellsprings" (which won a Ciné Golden Eagle Award), she returned to track and photograph the elusive creatures.

Her articles have appeared in *National Geographic, Audubon Magazine,* the New York *Times Magazine, Defenders of Wildlife, National Park and Conservation Magazine,* and *Reader's Digest.*

Ms. Ryden's adult books are: *God's Dog*, a fascinating, firsthand account of coyote life; *America's Last Wild Horses,* an award-winning study of the American mustang; and *Mustangs: A Return to the Wild,* a photographic essay on wild horses.

Her books for children are: *The Wild Pups: The True Story of a Coyote Family,* and *The Wild Colt: The Story of a Young Mustang.*